· VOYAGE TO THE BUNNY PLANET ·

# THE
# ISLAND LIGHT

## Rosemary Wells

DIAL BOOKS FOR YOUNG READERS
NEW YORK

Published by Dial Books for Young Readers
A Division of Penguin Books USA Inc.
375 Hudson Street • New York, New York 10014

THE BUNNY PLANET IN HISTORY
*I designated this heavenly body "Coniglio,"*
*but alas, never saw it again.*
Galileo (Diary entry, January 1, 1599)

Felix was sick in front of the whole art class.

The nurse made him a cup of tea and called home.
Nobody answered the phone.
Felix burned his tongue on the tea.

That afternoon the doctor gave Felix medicine
that tasted like gasoline.
Felix's mother and the nurse had to hold him
down for a shot.

Later Felix was accidentally soaked by an icy shower.

Felix's father was busy in the cellar with the boiler.
Felix's mother was busy finding a plumber.
Both forgot to kiss him good night.

Felix needs a visit to the Bunny Planet.

Far beyond the moon and stars,
Twenty light-years south of Mars,

Spins the gentle Bunny Planet
And the Bunny Queen is Janet.

"Felix," Janet says. "Come in.

Here's the day that should have been."

The mailboat comes at six o'clock.
I walk my father to the dock.

The boat brings apples, milk, and flour,
And sails back home within the hour.

A squall is stirring up the sky.
Our lighthouse home is warm and dry.

The light was built in nineteen-ten.
It's had six keepers here since then.

We're wet and salty, but who cares?
Our sweaters dry on kitchen chairs.

We mix an apple pancake batter,
Singing while the shutters clatter.

The night wind howls. The rain leaks in.
After supper we play gin.

Our sweaters steam. The fire crackles.
The ocean swells and lifts its hackles.

We split a piece of gingerbread
And play another round in bed.

Outside the sea enfolds the sand.
Inside I hold my father's hand.

*Felix wakes at midnight.*
*Out his bedroom window he sees the Bunny Planet*
*near the Milky Way in the summer sky.*
*"It was there all along!" says Felix.*